Roxy the Reindeer's Magical Christmas Journey

Inspiration: bedtime story for Ethan

And remembering our own Roxy

Written by Mike Provenzano

www.mikeprov.com

Illustrated by Colleen Grant

ISBN: 978-1-66780-119-3

Printed in the United States of America

First Edition

**Roxy is a reindeer
that lives at the North Pole.**

**Roxy has always dreamed
of pulling Santa's sleigh.**

However, Roxy was a very sad reindeer.
She has always wanted to pull
Santa's sleigh on Christmas Eve.

Roxy felt very alone in her stable, thinking about how her friends were going to travel around the world, flying through the sky, helping Santa deliver presents to all the good girls and boys.

She wasn't chosen
to pull
Santa's sleigh
along with
her other reindeer
friends again
this year.

Roxy fell asleep that night, but her reindeer friends were too excited to sleep as they thought about tomorrow night's trip.

One of Santa's reindeer, Colly, hurt her foot and was now unable to take the trip on Christmas Eve.

Santa shouts "Roxy, I have some very important news for you!!" but Roxy kept on sleeping with her reindeer snore. Santa tried to wake Roxy again, but he was unable to.

Santa leaves the stables and goes back to his workshop to prepare for Christmas Eve.

The next day, Roxy woke up to find sleighbells and garland all around her stable where she was sleeping, but she didn't know why they were there.

Once Roxy found out the good news she joined the other reindeer to prepare for their special journey.

Roxy is so happy she can't control her joy as she says

Santa asks Roxy if she would like to lead the team along with her best friend Savvy.

Roxy was very happy pulling Santa's Sleigh with all her friends!

Roxy flies from house to house with all her friends and is happy as can be!!

Everyone at the North Pole welcomes Santa and his team after a long night delivering presents!!

One by one, Santa delivers a special present to each of the reindeer on his team this year.

Roxy loves her present and thanks Santa. She then falls fast asleep smiling after her long day.

Roxy has loved her
Magical Christmas journey!!

About the Author

Mike is a father to 4 boys first and foremost!! He is also an award winning actor & producer / spokesperson / model / voiceover artist. From commercial, legit and spokesperson work to modeling, Mike is known for saying things like "I truly feel blessed to be a part of this industry." During these challenging times that we are all facing together, Mike finds it important to continue to be creative and more importantly, help others to continue to be creative as well. From using technology (Mike's background before becoming an actor) to connect with and work with others, Mike has kept busy both creating projects and bringing people together through unique projects.

Mike's mission in life is quite simple, to support his family as a full time actor and to help others in any way that he can along his journey. We all need support from time to time, so if it's through offering advice or connecting people together, one of Mike's greatest joys is inspiring others to be all they can.

About the Illustrator

Colleen is a graphic designer, painter, illustrator, and artist. She is currently attending West Chester University of Pennsylvania as a member of the Honors College as well as the College of Art and Design. She is always looking for another fun adventure or project to get involved in. Colleen is fueled by her desire to learn and try new things, whether it be a new art medium, or a new drink at her favorite tea shop.

Colleen has experience in being one of the main graphic designers for all of her former high school's needs. She also spent time working on a voting platform made by West Chester University students as the chief graphic designer. In the future, she looks forward to new and exciting creative ventures!

2021